Charles M. Schulz

Happy Halloween, Great Pumpkin!

Charles M. Schulz

HarperHorizon
An Imprint of HarperCollinsPublishers

First published in 1998 by HarperCollins*Publishers* Inc. http://www.harpercollins.com. Copyright © 1998 United Feature Syndicate, Inc. All rights reserved. HarperCollins ® and ♣ ® are trademarks of HarperCollins*Publishers* Inc. *Happy Halloween, Great Pumpkin!* was published by HarperHorizon, an imprint of HarperCollins*Publishers* Inc., 10 East 53rd Street, New York, NY 10022. Horizon is a registered trademark used under license from Forbes Inc. PEANUTS is a registered trademark of United Feature Syndicate, Inc. PEANUTS © United Feature Syndicate, Inc. Based on the PEANUTS ® comic strip by Charles M. Schulz. http://www.unitedmedia.com. ISBN 0-694-01054-5. Printed in Hong Kong.

"Halloween is coming, Marcie. Linus told me that on Halloween night the Great Pumpkin rises out of the pumpkin patch and brings gifts to all the kids in the world!"

"Guess who's sitting in a pumpkin patch . . . Peppermint Patty! You've finally got one, Linus!"

"A disciple!"

"You're going to be so excited, Patty."

"When the Great Pumpkin rises out of the pumpkin patch on Halloween night, it's a sight to behold!"

"Don't ask! Only the Great Pumpkin can make that judgment!"

"Wow!"

"Tomorrow is Halloween."

"Tomorrow I get my baseball glove!"

"Your what?"

"My baseball glove! I asked the Great Pumpkin to bring me a new glove."

"You don't *ask* the Great Pumpkin for a present! You wait for whatever he brings you! Don't you know how sensitive he is? What do you think he is, some kind of Santa Claus?"

"You've done the worst thing a person can do! You've offended the Great Pumpkin and the spirit of Halloween!"

"Banished from the pumpkin patch!"
Sigh.

"Do you know what happened to me, Peppermint Patty? I went trick-or-treating last night, and all I got in my bag was a rock!"

"I sat in a pumpkin patch for a week, and I didn't get anything!"

The snow is finally melting. We move back
up the mountain again.

I'm big enough to climb trees now. I spend most of my
day up here, eating and sleeping. Mom is always close by.

18

Two summers and winters pass. I have learned
everything I need to know from my mother.
It's time for me to find my own patch of forest.

20

Another panda comes to visit me.
He sings to me all day long. I bark a reply.

Soon, a new panda arrives.
My friend charges at him, scaring him away.

24

I now have a cub of my own. We play together in our patch of forest, rolling and tumbling. Soon I will teach him everything my own mother taught me.

DID YOU KNOW?

Baby pandas are tiny.

A newborn panda cub weighs about 3 ounces (85 g) and is about the length of a pencil. The mother is around 900 times the size of her baby! The cub has pink skin and small amounts of fuzzy fur. It cannot see or hear.

Mothers carry young cubs in their mouths, like cats do with kittens.

At around three weeks, the mother takes her cub with her when she goes into the forest to feed. She hides the cub in a patch of bamboo while she eats.

Cubs begin to walk at 3 to 4 months.

For the first three months, pandas can only move by rolling from side to side. They lie on their backs and kick their legs in the air. Their first steps are very wobbly. They also practice their tree-climbing skills, using their mother as a "climbing frame."

Pandas mainly eat bamboo.

Bamboo makes up 99 percent of a panda's diet. It is not very nutritious, so pandas need to spend up to 12 hours a day eating to get enough energy to live. On average, each day an adult panda will eat several hundred bamboo stalks, weighing about 27 pounds (12 kg).

Pandas have few predators.

Because of their large size, pandas have few predators. They are able to protect themselves and their cubs against attack with their claws and strong jaws. However, snow leopards, weasels, foxes, wild dogs and martens may eat unguarded cubs.

Unlike other bears, pandas do not hibernate in the winter.

Because bamboo is available all year round, pandas do not need to hoard food, hibernate or travel seasonally to find it. However, they often move down to the lower slopes and valleys where the air is warmer in winter.

Did You Know? (continued)

Pandas scent mark their territory.

Pandas mark their territory by spraying urine or rubbing their anal glands on trees or rocks. Sometimes they perform handstands so they can leave their mark as high up a tree branch as possible. This lets other pandas know to keep away from their food supply.

Cubs spend a lot of their day in trees.

Panda cubs begin to climb trees at around five months. They grip the branches with their sharp claws and haul themselves up. Trees provide a place to play and sleep as well as protection from predators.

Pandas are solitary animals.

Cubs stay with their mother for about two years, learning the skills they will need to survive on their own. After this they leave to find their own home range to live in. The only time they look for other pandas is when they are ready to mate.

Male pandas compete with each other at mating time.

Male and female pandas come together to mate in the spring. The male then leaves the female to raise the cub on her own. Males may need to travel a long way to find a female panda as their habitat is shrinking.

Female pandas are good mothers.

After giving birth, female pandas hold their cubs almost constantly. They don't leave the birth den to get food or water for themselves till the cub is a week old. Mothers sleep sitting up with their cub in their arms. As it grows older, a mother panda gives her cub lots of cuddles and encouragement.

MEET THE BEAR FAMILY

Giant pandas are bears. Here are some of their other family members:

Sun bear

Grizzly bear

Polar bear

QUIZ

1. Which of these bears is the largest?

2. Which is the smallest?

3. Which bears have black and white fur?

4. Which bear would be hard to spot against snow?

30

Giant panda

Scientific name: *Ailuropoda melanoleuca*

Coat color: White with distinctive black patches

Height: Up to 5 feet (1.5 m)

Weight: Up to 355 pounds (160 kg)

Life-span: 15–20 years in the wild

Diet: 99 percent bamboo

Habitat: Isolated bamboo forests in the mountains of southwestern and central China

Conservation status: Endangered (estimates vary from 1,500 to 3,000 in the wild)

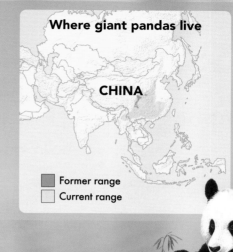

Where giant pandas live

CHINA

Former range
Current range

Giant panda

Red panda

Asiatic black bear

European brown bear

5. Which bears have white markings on their upper chest?

6. Which bear has a stripy tail?

7. Which bear looks the most scary?

A: 1. Polar bear 2. Red panda 3. Sun bear, Asiatic black bear, giant panda 4. Polar bear 5. Sun bear, Asiatic black bear 6. Red panda 7. Grizzly bear!

GLOSSARY

bamboo
a kind of giant grass with tough, hollow, woody stems

charge
to rush at

den
a cave or tree hollow where a giant panda gives birth then looks after her cub in its first weeks

grasslands
land covered with grass rather than shrubs and trees

mark
to leave an odor on a tree or rock to show its territory and warn other pandas to stay away

shoots
the new growth of a plant

snow leopard
a large cat from central Asia with long, thick, white fur

squeal
to make a high-pitched howl

stream
a small river

Published in 2017 by **Windmill Books**, an Imprint of Rosen Publishing
29 East 21st Street, New York, NY 10010

Copyright © 2017 Weldon Owen

All rights reserved. No part of this book may be reproduced in any form without permission in writing from the publisher, except by a reviewer.

Creative Director Sue Burk
Managing Editor Averil Moffat
Senior Editor Barbara McClenahan
Consultant Dr. George McKay
Design Concept Cooling Brown Ltd
Designer Gabrielle Green
Images Manager Trucie Henderson
Illustrations Stuart Jackson Carter
    except Meet the Bear Family pages.

Cataloging-in-Publication Data

Names: Costain, Meredith. | Jackson-Carter, Stuart, illustrator.
Title: Panda / Meredith Costain; illustrated by Stuart Jackson-Carter.
Description: New York : Windmill Books, 2017. | Series: Wild world
Identifiers: ISBN 9781508192893 (pbk.) | ISBN 9781499482218 (library bound) | ISBN 9781508193067 (6 pack)
Subjects: LCSH: Giant panda--Juvenile literature.
Classification: LCC QL737.C214 C69 2017 | DDC 599.789--d23

Manufactured in the United States of America

CPSIA Compliance Information: Batch #BW17PK: For Further Information contact Rosen Publishing, New York, New York at 1-800-237-9932